Let me tell you a story

Let me tell you a story

A collection of short fiction and poems with their own author soundtracks

Edited by Suzanne Conboy-Hill

First published by Waif Sands Publishing 2016

808.81

Copyright © 2016 S.P. Conboy-Hill. All rights reserved. This book or any portion thereof may not be reproduced or used in any manner whatsoever without the expressed written permission of the publisher except for the use of brief quotations in a book review or scholarly journal.

First printing 2016

ISBN 978-1-326-63962-4

Suzanne Conboy-Hill asserts her right to be acknowledged as the originator of the unique text/audio/QR code combination and owner of Readalongreads © 2016 and its derivatives

Published by WAIF SANDS PUBLISHING, Sussex, UK in association with Readalongreads.
Waif.sands@outlook.com

Cover by Suzanne Conboy-Hill

Acknowledgments

Jess Moriarty, Ines Garcia, Graham Mort; all the contributors for taking a leap in the dark; and anyone looking to dispel the 'language mist'[1] of the written word.

---

[1] Ian McMillan, page vi

Foreword

I Hear What You Say

WORDS ON THE page have their own dynamic. They have shape and pattern, they have a kind of rhythmic beauty and they have meaning; sometimes, though, the meaning is lost in clouds of misunderstanding. You can't fathom what a word means, you don't quite get what the writer is getting at, you feel they're simply writing into the air and the words aren't settling anywhere near you, and if they do settle you approach them and they fly away like startled birds. As a reader, you get frustrated. You think that you and the writer are on different streets, different continents, different planets.

The air, though, the air: that's where this project comes in, because that's where the writing in this book will live. Or rather, it will live in the space between the eye and the ear, the space where understanding often happens.

The idea is that this is a new approach to reading, and a new approach to listening, and these approaches lead to somewhere different and exciting. Each of the pieces of writing in this book have their own soundtrack; the soundtrack emphasises and illuminates the writing and somehow it makes the reading experience greater than the sum of its parts.

Sometimes I can read a poem on the page and I can't quite make out what the author's intention was: there's something there, I can tell, but it's hidden in the language-mist. When I hear the poem read aloud, (or accompanied by music, or acted out by a variety of voices: anything is possible once you start down this road) then the clouds are blown away and the poem does what it meant to say on the tin, to re-fashion an advertising slogan. Sometimes, because I'm not a very practical man, my eyes and my brain will glaze over when I'm reading a set of technical instructions and subsequently the thing I'm assembling doesn't work, or works for a minute and then staggers to a halt. If I could be listening to the instructions as I read them then the meaning would become abundantly clear and the thing I'm assembling would work forever.

Clarity, then, is at the heart of this project. To read a piece of writing and hear the soundtrack of the words at the same time will be a real boon for people for whom accessing the language doesn't come easy, for whatever reason. The writer and the reader will be in the same place, meeting eye to eye. Meaning (that word again: I'm using it a lot but it's important, it's really important) becomes clear.

Now it's up to you: try the experiment. Read the pieces in this book and listen to the soundtracks. Listen to the readings and the voice will underline the words on the page and will make them stand out in three dimensions. Reading will not work for a minute and then stagger to a halt. Using this method, reading will work forever.

Ian McMillan, poet, broadcaster, comedian, and presenter of BBC R3's *The Verb*.
© Ian McMillan
@IMcMillan

Photo credit Andy Boag

Preface

MAYBE YOU LOVE having stories read to you, or you find poetry makes no sense until you hear it performed. Maybe you're reading English as a second language and it would help to hear the pronunciation, the tone and rhythm of words as you follow along on the page. Or perhaps reading is a bit of a struggle sometimes, especially when there are unfamiliar words that trip you up and put you off wanting to read on. When you lose reading fluency, meaning goes too, and what story can possibly fire the imagination if its meaning is lost?

If any of that rings true, this book might be right up your street because here every story or poem is accompanied by a sound track you can listen to on your smart device. This means you can take it anywhere there's an internet connection and hear the authors' own voices as you read.

But why would you do that? Why not just listen, save the bother of reading? Well, you can of course, you can do whatever you like, but reading while you listen gives you a unique opportunity to make links between the shapes of words and their sounds, something an audio book can't do.

Listening to the sound tracks as you follow along silently to yourself lets you hear troublesome or unfamiliar words sounded out with the emphasis the writer wanted them to have. You'll feel the pace, the stops and starts and rhythms they put there to give the story its mood and flavour, and then there's that layer of magic that comes from having something read to you as you sit in a café, on the beach, the bus, anywhere you like, plugged in with your book on your knee.

The voices you will hear are all female although that is not by design. Some are British, others South African, Irish, and Vietnamese; all with different pitches and styles and all reading stories or poems they crafted themselves.

The content is equally varied: there is the everyday realism of relationships – lost ones, disintegrating ones, cheeky sassy ones, ones undergoing renewal. There's growing up, ageing, and observation of the trajectories of others' lives. There's humour, science fiction, and fantasy.

Some of the works though make direct reference to catastrophic events such as the ongoing impact of the war in Vietnam, the civil war in Colombia, and the shock of an air show jet ploughing into stationary traffic, and dedicate their words to the ordinary people so profoundly affected.

To hear the sound tracks, you need a smart device such as an iPhone, Android or similar, with a free QR scanner[3] app installed. Scanning the code at the top of each story takes you to the *Readalongreads*[4] [5] site where the tracks are stored. When the page loads, you'll be asked for a password; there's one for each story or poem and you'll find it under title. All you have to do then is type it in, pop in your earbuds, and let us tell you some stories.

Suzanne Conboy-Hill

---

[3] There are several available, free to download and to use.
[4] *Readalongreads* hosts the files for Let Me Tell You a Story and invites other writers, especially from the health and scientific communities where communication with the public is critical, to use the site on a trial basis for their own product.
[5] In the event that Readalongreads is unable to maintain its role as host OR towards the end of the lifetime of the book, voice files will become available as free downloads.

Contents

Anne O'Brien 1
   A Soft Day 2
Lyn Jennings 11
   Red Whirlwind 13
   Heatwave 16
   Not Going Out 19
   Shadow 21
Tracy Fells 25
   Phoenix and Marilyn 26
   Wood 34
   Tantric Twister 40
Nguyen Phan Que Mai 43
   Tears of Quang Tri 45
   Mrs Moreno 47
   The Colour of Peace 49
   On Hanoi Street 51
Suzanne Conboy-Hill 53
   Puddles like Pillows 54
   Albert's Teeth 59
   Terminus 61

    When Gliese Met Glasgow (and Muira made a mint) 63

    The Collector 68

    Ducks in a Row 71

Phillippa Yaa de Villiers 75

    Bones 78

    Breastsummer 80

    Rapture 82

    Origin 85

Credits 87

Anne O'Brien

ANNE O'BRIEN IS an Irish writer living in Brussels. She is a graduate of the Lancaster university MA in Creative Writing, and is currently working towards a PhD there. She has had several stories published and also shortlisted or placed in many competitions including for the Bridport Prize and the BBC's Opening Lines

Photo credit Hannah O'Brien-Møller

A Soft Day[7]
aob1sof

THE RAIN RUNS in muddy rivulets off the pile of earth beside his grave. No softening of the edges of this funeral. No fake grass discretely covers the mound, just a heap of mud, a pair of dirty spades, and two reluctant gravediggers in fluorescent jackets leaning against the neighbouring gravestone, silently willing us to move on so they can get the job done and head to the pub. Of course nothing will do the Ma but she has to wait until the last shovelful is put on. They pat down the soil with the backs of their spades as though they're on a building site.

'Don't worry that it's a bit high Missus. It'll settle down grand in the next few weeks...'

Settle down on top of him and in time, when the wood rots and the earth seeps in, settle down until it kisses his face. I wish I'd kissed him now.

We place the wreaths on the grave as the rain buckets down,

---

[7] Included in the Baker Prize Anthology, *A Stillness of Mind*, 2014. Ed Linda Cracknell

'*Sincere condolences from all at Fahey's.*' I tear the card off and stuff it my damp pocket before she sees it.

'A decent man', they said after the Mass, 'never had a harsh word for anyone...'

Fahey's, the bookies. She'd have a fit.

'Would you look at that?' she says, pointing at a plastic dome of artificial roses. 'Isn't that only gorgeous? The others will be gone off in a few days but that'll keep grand.'

She cries as we leave the graveyard. Father Pat puts his black crow's arm around her and says the Da is looking down on her from heaven. I streel behind them, kicking stones.

Back home and the house seems to have shrunk while we were out. The neighbours drink endless cups of tea and eye us like new exhibits at the zoo. The weirdest thing is that the Da seems more alive now that he's dead. Ma has given him a voice he never had. Pat goes along with it, or 'Father Pat' as I'm supposed to call him since his ordination.

'Oh what a day that was, I'm so glad your father lived to see it, his own son, a priest.'

He too leaves Da's chair empty and sits looking at it as though he can see him in the indent forged by his bum. They've re-invented him, into a saint that wouldn't be seen dead in the bookies – wouldn't be seen dead, ha! I can see the way it's going, his shoes will be left standing inside the door as though he's just stepped out of them, his place empty at the table. Soon he'll start to have opinions about things he never cared less about.

'I'll have a lick of paint put on the front room in the summer, please God. Green, I think, Daddy likes green,' she'll say.

The house empties and the neighbours leave a silence behind them.

'I'll head off for a bit of a spin,' I say. 'Get a breath of fresh air.'

'Sure I'll come with you,' says Pat, raising his eyes from his clasped hands.

'No,' I say quickly, 'you keep the Ma company.'

'Will you be back for a bite to eat?' she says.

'Ye go-ahead, I'll pick up something.'

I head out the door as her voice trails behind me.

'Sure where would he be going at this hour?'

I leave them to it, sitting each side of the fireplace. I get out quick before the urge to plonk myself in his chair overwhelms me, the thought of the shock on their faces, as though he died all over again and was lying squashed under me arse.

I get in the car and join the last of the commuters heading home. The traffic thins out and in no time I see the tops of the deserted caravans through the bare trees. Here already? It was so far when we were young. The days it took to pack up for the long trip to the caravan for the holidays, the holiday really only starting when the Da sat down, undid his shoelaces, peeled off his socks and pushed his white feet deep into the sand.

I park the car and head down to the sea, the pebbles crunching under my feet. I walk along the water's edge until my legs ache and I'm soaked through, then I turn inland and head toward lights at the end of an overgrown lane. Blessed Ireland, no matter where you are, you're never far from a pub.

It's quiet and dim inside. A woman, *no spring chicken*, as the Da would say, sits alone at the bar, her eyes on the door. She nods and pulls out the stool beside her. I look behind me as the door murmurs shut. She pats the seat and I sit down. The barman shifts, pulling a disinterested dishcloth over the counter.

'What'll it be?'

'A pint, and... whatever...?'

'Jackie,' she smiles. 'A glass of white – cold, mind.'

'Séan,' I say taking the seat beside her, giving the Da's name, 'Séan.' A couple of pints later and we're walking up the road to a row of bungalows ignoring the sea.

'You'll come in?' she says and I do.

'You're lovely Séan,' she says, draping her arms around my neck.

How could I do it, with the Da hardly cold in his grave? Stone cold more like it – there was nothing warm about that coffin despite the padded satin lining.

Stripping off, I catch sight of myself in her bathroom mirror. For fuck's sake, when did that happen? My body has settled just like his, my hips broad and soft, my neck ruddy against my chest with its greying hair.

Slap, slap – flesh on flesh, in the musty bedroom, with the thinly curtained windows letting in too much light for comfort. A couple of pints and somehow it had all seemed possible, exciting even. God forgive me. A few hours later I leave her, barefoot on the cold tiled floor in her beige kitchen, loneliness making her face mean, and her peach satin dressing gown looking the worse for wear.

'Go,' she says, 'Go on. Ye're all the same, only after the one thing.'

'Sorry,' I say pulling the door behind me, glad of the dark as I walk back to the car.

Is that it? A one night's stand in a bungalow in the middle of nowhere, is that all ye missed Da? I think of the double bed sagging in the middle and the puddle of the Ma's rosary beads on the bedside table. Did ye love her Da? Did ye?

I pull out onto the dual carriageway and point the car towards home. God, maybe they sat up all night waiting for me like the Ma used to when I staggered back from the school disco having drunk myself brave. I think of my dark suit and tie hanging on the back of the door in our childhood bedroom and 'Father' Pat snoring in the twin bed. I can't go back, I just can't. I press the pedal hard to the floor and the car strains as the radio belts out 1980's pop songs.

Even with the wipers on full, I can hardly see out the window. I lean over the steering wheel, my eyes on the tail lights of the car in front. Slap, slap go the wipers, letting me glimpse the clouds snagged on the peaks of the Wicklow Mountains. It never rains like this in Brussels. There are wet days, weeks even, when the sky hangs low and the clouds don't shift. But this is proper weather; lashing rain, clouds that can't hold their own against the buffeting wind and the knowledge that at any moment the break will come and the sun pierce through picking out the yellow gorse or a few sheep on the side of a hill. That gets me, every time.

Ashford village is still asleep, the pubs shuttered, the curtains drawn. The only light is from the small all night store in the garage. 'Áth na Fuinseoige' the sign says, not much of a ford now though, just the weir where the boggy waters of the Varty river disappear under the road. I leave it behind me and the road twists and turns through Glen of the Downs, the blanket of ancient oak and rowan forest on each side, shrouded in mist.

The sky lightens from the east and the shadows of the clouds are like great stains on the hills, the skinny legged sheep huddle into the mountain for shelter. The road climbs and I shift down a gear as the car labours. I reach the top and Dublin Bay is spread out below me, the lights of the city running down to the sea.

A few miles later, the steering wheel is wrenched to the left. I hobble onto the hard shoulder and get out. The front tyre is spread out each side of the wheel's rim. I get the tools and spare out of the boot and set to work pulling up my collar against the rain. Suddenly he's there, quietly pleased with the way I set up the jack and raise the wheel, just how he taught me.

'It'll be a soft day, thank God,' he says as he did many a time, thanking his maker for the sheets of misty rain on the hills, 'A grand soft day,' he'd say as he studied the form for the 3 o' clock race at Leopardstown.

'Turf soft too – aye,' shifting in his chair as he had marked the runners with his secret code, to be translated later into bets. Job done, he'd fold the paper into the pocket of his jacket.

'I'll be off out so Maura,' he'd say.

I loosen the wheel nuts thinking of the day he'd had a run of luck and slipped a five pound note into my hand.

'Say nothin',' he said nodding towards the kitchen.

'What'd you say we have fish and chips tonight, Maura?' rattling the coins in his pocket. She had come out, wiping her hands on her apron, suspicion and relief battling it out on her face, the lovely prospect of no dinner to cook.

'Go on then.'

'Will I come with you Da?'

'Do Lad,' he'd said and we headed down the road to Liberto's, stopping off at the local – a pint for himself, a rock shandy for me, sipped as we'd watched the re-runs of the Gaelic football finals on the big screen.

'That'll be you one day,' he said looking at the telly. 'Didn't I see you score a goal in the under 12's final, Croke Park, no less? I'll never forget that.' But that was never me, I followed in his footsteps, pushing a pen over paper in another office in another country.

We had headed across to the chippers for four singles and battered cod soaked in salt and vinegar and then the slow walk home. I worked a hole into the wrapping and the vinegary steam gushed out; the bliss of a boiling chip inched out and popped in the mouth, saliva rushing to meet it.

On the side of a road in the middle of nowhere, I sit back on my heels and laugh. The clouds shift and the rain stops and suddenly it's over. I lower the car and put the jack back in the boot, the taste of salt on my lips.

I'm going home.

Lyn Jennings

LYN HAS ALWAYS enjoyed reading, writing and, most of all, performing poems. At school she was such an enthusiast that she gained Distinction in every Speech and Drama exam she took. Instead, at her parents' insistence, she opted for teaching as a career, gaining the appropriate Degree and Certificate and following this with training as an Educational Psychotherapist which enabled her to work at a much deeper level with children with learning difficulties.

Lyn also holds a diploma in Counselling from The Central School of Counselling Training. and a Masters with Distinction in the Study of Counselling and the Therapeutic Potential of Creative Writing from the University of Hertfordshire. Her last post was as Senior Lecturer on the BA in Humanistic Counselling and the MA in Transpersonal Arts and Practice at the University of Chichester.

Photo credit Ian Black.

Lyn's poems have been published in Journals and a variety of books - Hearing Ourselves by Verena Tschudin and Counselling for Older People also by Verena Tschudin, and anthologies such as The Journal of Educational Therapy and New Christian Poetry.

Red Whirlwind
lj1red

LATE AUTUMN AFTERNOON

I walk by the beach,
sun is tucked behind
grey cushion clouds
sending spindly shafts
of silver light
to prick the surface of the sea,
a chill wind rattles the trees.

The children's playground
is deserted –
jumble of climbing ropes
a grotesque giant spider's web,
empty swings swaying slightly,
sad half-tilted seesaw,
painted rocking birds
cocking their beaks at the sky,
a faded wooden shark
stands awkwardly on its tail
big mouth stretched
in a menacing smile,
a trickle of sand flows
from a suspended bucket
as if pushed by a small hand.

Ghostly - quiet – empty,
     then
 a red whirlwind appears
he leaps over the wall,
nimble as a frenzied chimp
he claws his way swiftly
up the climbing frame
yelling and shouting as if
he must fill all this emptiness,
clomping from end to end of the seesaw
he makes it hit the ground
with a body -jolting thud,
he heaves the roundabout into motion
it turns slowly at first then gathers speed
he doesn't jump on but stands back,
watching and whooping,
glancing toward his mother,

"Mum look "

        he yells,

her eyes are fixed on her phone,

he pounds on ,
filling the hanging bucket with sand,
he gives it a great push, sending

clouds of the yellow grey dust
scattering in the wind,
he screams with delight,
standing on a swing,
he makes the chains rattle
and creak in their sockets,

"Look how
        high I am"
    he yells to his mother.

She doesn't look up,
eyes still on her phone.

I nod and smile at him
as I pass,
trying to fill the gap
of his mother's disinterest,
he stares at me
not smiling,

"Mum,
      mum" he pleads,
  "Look at me
    I'm going higher
     and higher,
         Mum, Mum!"

Heatwave
lj2wav

TAUT AS A CRYSTAL sheet
                    stretched across
                    the body of
                    the drowning land
                    the sea is mirage
                    in the shimmering haze
                    waves like the sighs
                    of a grieving widow
curdle softly up the beach
leaving a clean curve
in the dusty shingle,

sky cloudless,
as sun burns its way across
the fierce blue vastness,

at the edge of the sand
the necklace of huts
blisters in the heat,
flagstone patios
lolling like the tongues
of thirsty dogs,

pebbles cleaned

in the wash of water
glitter like hot coals

people hide
beneath bright parasols
frying gently
in their slathered oil
bodies crisping like
fresh- baked bread,
too hot to move,
while the receding tide
is sucked away leaving
crystal pools, the smell
of seaweed cooking in the sun,

the "cold drinks" sign
has been taken down
"sold out" softly creaking
 in its place,
the ice cream van
has slipped soundlessly away
leaving a melting slush
of raspberry ripple
dropped by a child
too hot to care,

deep in the distance
a drum roll of thunder

reverberates through hot bodies,
sky darkens,
lightning crackles
and the first few drops of rain
sizzle on the bonnets
of overheated cars.

Not Going Out.
lj3not

WHEN GRANDCHILDREN PERSIST
it's hard to resist
and insist that your bones are too
old,
that you can't find you scarf
or your hat or your gloves
and the weather might give you a
cold,
in your warm winter lair
there's the snare of the chair
and the pull of a full cup of tea,
there's the hook of a book
with its welter of words
and the drag of a programme to see,

when your head feels like lead,
there's the lure of the bed
and the snug of a rug on your knees,
then there's hot buttered toast
which you know you like most
with a smother of soft melted cheese,

you can see in your mind the reach of the beach
and imagine the sea as it pounds,
you can feel all the "shoulds"

from the Downs and the Woods,
you can hear all those wild winter sounds,

it's dark in the park with no people about,
there's a rattle of rain on the walls,
for now, without doubt
it's too late to go out
and the sight of a bright fire calls

Shadow[9]
lj4shad

SKY ACHINGLY BLUE
        empty of clouds
        sun a glowing ball making up for
        weeks of showers and cool winds,
        grass with that warm smell
        of fresh cut hay.

        People gathering,
cold boxes full of well-filled sandwiches and ice for drinks,
children running ahead,
doing those little skips
your legs need to do when you are young,
calling out to each other
excitement quivering in the air.

Older folk, sensing the nostalgia
that will take them back to skies awash
with planes - Spitfires, Hurricanes,

---

[9] Dedicated to our neighbours at Shoreham with respect and sympathy for all who died or suffered in the Air Show disaster.

today there's even a promise of a Vulcan.

Close your eyes, they say
and you could be back in the Andersen
listening to the hum of engines,
waiting for the whine of bombs, the thud
before the explosion,
tension clenching fists, making the gut churn
waiting for the throb of Spitfires,
or the welcome wolf howl of
the "all clear"
Days long gone, nothing to fear today,
comfy seat, glass of beer,
bit of shade from the sun,
it's going to be great!

Cars gleam in neat stripes
across the field,
everything well organised,
thousands here
masses still on the approach road,
let the show begin!

No-one
could have
known,
no-one
could have foreseen

the massive
shadow
that would darken
the so-bright day
looming across
the busy road
blotting out the sun,
great wallowing bird of prey,
struggling
to lift itself
out of its daring swoop and dive
Hurricane bird
losing the power of its wings,
coming in to land
too low
too soon
crashing
screaming
screeching its metal - wrenching way
across the crowded road
destroying   everything   in its path
shooting a great fireball
shrouded in black smoke
high into the   cobalt sky
turning joy
in a tragic instant
to terror and sadness,
   changing   lives   forever.

How could the sun
still be shining?
Why does the sky
tell us it is summer
when it feels as if winter has come?

In the pattern of planes
flying away from the airfield there is
a   great gap
throbbing   with   questions.

Tracy Fells

TRACY FELLS LIVES close to the beautiful South Downs in West Sussex. She has won awards for both fiction and drama. Her short stories are published in national magazines including *Firewords Quarterly*, online at *Litro New York* and in anthologies such as *Fugue* (Siren Press) and *Rattle Tales2*. Competition success includes short-listings for the Commonwealth Writers Short Story Prize, Fish Short Story and Flash Fiction Prizes. Currently, Tracy is seeking representation for her debut novel after receiving her MA in Creative Writing (Chichester University). She shares a blog with The Literary Pig (*http://tracyfells.blogspot.co.uk/*), haunts Facebook and tweets as @theliterarypig

---

Photo credit Graham Fells

Phoenix and Marilyn[11]
tf1nix

'ARE YOU SURE you want to go through with this?' Hannah paused, giving Lou a moment to consider, her fingertips tightly pinching the edge of the paper strip.

With eyes tightly closed her best friend nodded. 'Do it.' As Hannah tore the waxed paper downwards Lou let out a shriek, the piercing cry of a doomed creature caught in a snare.

'Told you it would hurt,' said Hannah, suppressing a smile. 'Do you want me to carry on?'

They both appraised the runway, a rectangle of white skin trailing from kneecap to shin, bounded by the remaining forest of chestnut hairs. 'You've got to do the rest – I can't go out looking like a half-skinned bear in a dress.'

Hannah patted the peroxide blonde curls of Lou's wig. Stretching up she arched her back and with a sigh she glanced at the wardrobe's full-length mirror. 'Is this

---

[11] *Phoenix and Marilyn* won 2012 ChocLit Publishing's Summer Short Story Prize.

really a good idea? You make one really ugly tart and I'm the vicar from hell.' Standing sideways in the black tunic and trousers, ecclesiastical collar and with her red spiky hair she looked like a pencil with a rubber glued on top - a skinny pencil with pale sunken cheeks and weary eyes.

'We could do with a night out. The consultant gave us the all clear, so I reckon we should be celebrating.' Lou held out the crimson lipstick, hands trembling and lips pouting like a carp poised for a kiss.

'Please let me do that,' Hannah wrenched the lipstick away. 'Then I'll finish the defuzzing. I just hope everyone else read Suzy's invitation properly and realises this is a fancy dress Bonfire party.' She studied her partner closely, watching the stuffed out fake cleavage rise and fall with each stilted breath. 'Are you sure you're up to it? You've been through a lot these last months. You look tired, love.'

Lou kissed the warm centre of her palm. 'We've both been through a lot, Hannah. Now it's time to party. I am tired, but I'm looking forward to showing off my curves in this dress. All eyes will be on me.' Thick black eyelashes winked at her, waving like the tentacles of a sea monster. The glue hadn't quite set and the lashes stuck together fast. Lou's remaining open eye began to water.

The last ten months had been torturous with several dark days when Hannah doubted they had any future together. But the disease had retreated, hounded into remission by the savage twins of chemo and radiation. The all clear signalled a blessing, gave them permission to start planning again, permission to live again.

'Yep,' Hannah kissed the bridge of Lou's nose between the swirling, unkempt brows, 'all eyes will definitely be on you.'

Hannah didn't doubt it. Who would notice the skeletal vicar with a ghoulish complexion when there was a thirteen stone, six foot Marilyn Monroe in strappy heels and a bulging satin frock to ogle?

*

Suzy jiggled the half empty bottle of red wine, grinning widely she asked, 'So who's the designated driver tonight?'

Lou covered the plastic cup with his hand. 'That's me, I'm afraid.'

Suzy tipped the bottle towards Hannah's cup, but she also slipped her hand across to block the wine. 'I can drive home,' said Hannah quickly, 'I still have no appetite for alcohol. You can have a drink, love.'

Lou turned away from the bonfire, his cheeks glowing. An arm slipped around Hannah's sharp waist as he growled, 'I'm driving'.

'Ooh, not in those heels I hope,' squealed Suzy. She nodded down to Lou's silver stilettos studded with diamonds. 'They're gorgeous, where did you get them?'

'Where does one buy size eleven evening shoes dripping with bling?' Hannah jumped in. 'Luckily we found this great trannie website, in fact we got the whole ensemble from there.'

Suzy leant in towards the couple, her voice excited. 'And have you set a date yet?'

Hannah stroked a finger over the engagement ring; the stones glinted in the flickering light of the bonfire. 'We thought we'd wait another six months, at least, just to make sure. Then we can start planning the wedding.'

Lou squeezed her hand. 'I think we should book the wedding now, get in before Christmas. In fact Christmas Eve would be my choice.'

'A Christmas wedding,' Suzy would have gleefully clapped her hands if she hadn't been clutching the wine bottle, 'how romantic.'

'I was rather hoping to ditch Phoenix first. Wanted to see her go into the flames,' said Hannah with a weak smile. 'You know, rebirth and all that.'

'Phoenix is her pet name for the wig,' explained Lou. Hannah slipped her hand from his to self-consciously pat at the stiff red hair on her head. 'And this is a perfect opportunity to burn the past. Why not make use of this excellent bonfire?' Lou reached up and tugged at his tight blonde curls. 'Marilyn can keep Phoenix company if you like.'

Suzy gasped as Lou pulled off his Marilyn wig to reveal a shaven scalp. The dragon tongue flames of the bonfire seemed to lick at the smooth, polished surface of Lou's head.

'Oh, Louie, what have you done?' cried Hannah. She wanted to touch his beautiful brown curls, but they had vanished. He was completely bald.

'I wanted to keep you company.' He held out the peroxide wig towards the bonfire. 'If Marilyn goes into the flames then Phoenix has to go too.'

Suzy let out another squeal, but this time her surprise was directed towards the patio and the buffet table. 'Sorry, Hannah, I forgot to warn you about Chloe's new boyfriend. She's started seeing Matt.'

'Not Matt Harker?' said Hannah, already knowing the answer.

Lou sucked in his cheeks and then spat out a rude word. Hannah's ex, elegantly dressed in a dark period suit with ivory waistcoat, was about to squirt ketchup onto his open burger. 'Count Dracula is rather lame fancy dress,' he said snidely.

'Actually he's come as Mr Darcy,' said Suzy. She air kissed Hannah's cheek and began to shrink away, sidestepping like a shameful crab. 'Must circulate, sweeties, catch you later.'

'Figures,' muttered Lou. 'He does the tall, dark handsome hero cliché so well.' A satin strap slunk off his slouching shoulder as his head bowed forward.

Hannah eyed her ex-boyfriend and sent up a little prayer, hoping for ketchup splash back right across his silk cravat and matching waistcoat. 'He's a prat,' she said simply. 'And you can tell a real hero from his deeds, not from his looks.'

Beside her loomed a large, muscular man trying to retain his balance on tottering dagger-sharp heels. His bulky frame oozed out of the dress in all the wrong places, while his newly shaven head gleamed like a beacon. Lou knew her reluctance to wear Phoenix out in public, understood how she felt about her sallow skin and loss of curves. His Marilyn outfit had been a superb ploy, skilfully executed, to draw attention away from Hannah. Nobody had commented on her appearance when there were easy jokes to be made at Lou's expense.

'You're all man, Louie,' said Hannah leaning up to kiss him on glossy lips, 'and I love you.' With a bony finger she caught his tear.

She swept off the wig and skimmed it like a pebble into the bonfire. Lou brushed his lips over the soft fox red fuzz covering her head, kissed her crown and then threw the Marilyn wig into the flames. The two wigs twisted together as if locked in a bizarre mating ritual.

'Marilyn and Phoenix embracing in death,' said Lou.

'Only to be reborn from the ashes,' added Hannah. 'Imagine what wondrous creature will emerge. Anything is possible.'

'Fancy marrying me on Christmas Eve?' he whispered.

The bald man in a frock was her lover, best friend and fiancé. He could soon become her husband too. 'Yeah,' she couldn't help the grin, 'go on then.'

Before they left the party Hannah returned to the dying bonfire. The two wigs had shrivelled into one blackened mass, no longer recognisable as Phoenix and Marilyn. The acrid smell of singed hair blew across the garden. Ashes floated above her in the night sky like grey snowflakes. Beneath the smouldering debris Hannah thought she saw a glint of white, the dome of a shell, as if a fire bird had laid its precious single egg in the bowels of the bonfire.

Wood[12]
tf2woo

RICHARD WATCHED THE flame burn black, as the final candle's wick sank to the base of the flimsy tea light. The other four were already garish green puddles, remnants of last Christmas dug out hastily to illuminate the evening.

'There's sorbet for pudding,' said Sarah, leaning across the heavy tang of wilting pine to take Richard's plate.

'I love your lemon sorbet,' he replied.

'Shop bought. Sorry. Didn't have time.' Her words burbled like a burst pipe.

Richard dabbed his lips with a linen serviette, one of six, wedding gifts from her parents and embroidered with their entwined initials. 'Still a "yes" to the sorbet. Shall I make coffee?'

'If you like.' Sarah was already carrying the dishes to the kitchen. Flat, still damp hair dripped

---

[12] *Wood* was shortlisted for 2015 The Fiction Desk Flash Fiction Prize

towards the curve of her back, the tangled ends, over long and splitting.

'How about an early night?' He called out hopefully.

Her voice echoed back from the kitchen, 'I'd prefer to watch some telly, relax for a bit. It's been a hell of a day. I'm shattered, but not ready for bed yet.'

Richard picked up the new pepper grinder; almost a foot high, polished and gleaming like an ebony phallic totem. Was his wife's anniversary gift a comment on his emotional intelligence, implying his inner life was static, immobile as a dense, dark forest? Or was she just taking the piss out of his manhood?

'We needed a replacement,' Sarah had stated, 'and it *is* made of wood. Five years is the wooden anniversary.'

'Oh. I didn't know that.'

He should have played her at her own game; presented a tray of ice cubes, carefully wrapped in scented tissue paper, instead of the exorbitantly expensive bra and knickers set he'd chosen late that afternoon. The bra cups, or what masqueraded as support, were too small. *Apparently*. But how he could know her cup size when he rarely penetrated the perimeter petticoat?

The jingle of cutlery and slap of plates signalled Sarah was loading the dishwasher. Richard waited for her to return with the sorbet, not technically a pudding more of a palate cleansing head freeze.

'Prefer to watch telly, huh,' he muttered. Anticipating his wife's lack-lustre libido Richard had a contingency plan ready for execution. In the gloom he slit open the sachet with a steak knife and tipped half the contents into his glass. The other half went into Sarah's untouched Merlot. Richard swilled the crystal goblet to dissolve the clear stringy droplets. He drank the rest of his wine quickly. Sharp and stringent it burned the back of his throat. Maybe he should've pushed the boat out a little further and picked up some bubbly. Prosecco used to work a treat on Sarah's underwear.

'Can I help?' he called out.

'No.' She swung back through the door with two dishes, one in each hand. 'I can manage.' Sarah's voice lightened, 'Where did you pick up the roses, the supermarket?'

'Don't you like them?'

Two yellow spheres of sorbet, suns in miniature, squatted in the cereal bowl she placed before him. Richard felt the crack of ice at the edge of his spoon. The CD had ended. Neither of them moved to restart or replace it.

'Somebody's cocked up big time.' She smirked, letting out a hiccup. 'The sachet of nutrients that came with the roses - it does a lot more sustaining than normal.' Richard blinked, as the room began to drift out of focus. Sarah tossed an empty black packet onto the tablecloth. *'Put the sex back into your romance,'* she said and giggled. 'I don't know what I've just emptied into the flower vase but I think it's supposed to do more than stiffen their stems.'

He could no longer reply, mouth clogged with twigs and leaf litter, and his throat crackled, studded with musty bark.

'Some idiot's muddled up the packets; whether by accident or for a joke, but it appears your half dozen blooms came with a sachet of love juice. What a hoot!' Sarah knelt beside him, rhythmically stroking the material of his trousers.

A dank coldness like ancient roots pushed down through his chest, down through his static legs, through his socks, through the soles of his feet into the thick cream carpet.

'I'm feeling more relaxed now,' whispered Sarah. 'Why don't you bring the rest of the wine upstairs and we can have that early night after all? I'll just go up and change.'

Richard couldn't raise his head to watch her leave, unable to twist or turn his thick, solid neck. She hadn't spotted the other, empty, sachet the one that had come with the flowers, the one he'd picked up in haste. Around him the house settled quietly, cooling and contracting.

Sarah returned wearing only a petticoat. White satin stretched across the swell of her breasts and belly. Richard felt vindicated; she had put on weight.

'I've been waiting.' The girlish giggle had gone. Sarah's mouth was a tight pink line. 'Why are you still sitting in the dark?'

Lignin oozed through his veins, leaching beyond capillaries into every cell, coating every synapse. Memories scurried away like deserting rats, leaving Richard oddly relieved. The burden of sentient existence, of responsibility and guilt, would soon be extinguished. He could just *be*.

'I wanted to tell you something tonight,' said Sarah, her eyes squinting. 'Something important. About us. About our future.' Pale hands cradled the curve of her stomach.

A small remembrance of Richard flickered. His seed had fallen on fertile ground.

'You really are a prick.' She snatched up the pepper grinder. 'I'd get more response from this wooden object. You're sleeping in the spare room tonight, okay!'

The pepper grinder flew over Richard's head, bounced off the wall, and bowled the photograph frame off the mantelpiece into the fireplace, where the glass splintered on the slate tiles, freeing the two startled mannequins from their wedding day pose.

Somewhere, deep inside his trunk, a nerve ending twitched.

Tantric Twister[13]
tf3twi

THE MIDSUMMER SUN penetrates the conservatory, amber shafts of light slipping between the polished slats of the wooden blinds. Judy backs up to Peter so he can unhook her bra. The white straps fall easily from her chestnut shoulders. Her tossed-aside blouse hides the bashful eyes of cuddly toys, corralled and tidied onto the bamboo sofa.

As Judy wriggles off denim slacks, followed by simple cotton panties, Peter's concentration skips to a lone yellow Lego brick on the plastic sheet. He must remember to put it away. The imprint of Lego in soft flesh was a typical hazard on Thursday evenings.

She tugs the navy polo shirt over his head and unbuckles his belt. Her bifocals dangle, bouncing off creamy breasts. For most of the afternoon the baby had fixated on the glinting links of the chain, plump pink fingers grasping, only succumbing to sleep for the last

---

[13] *Tantric Twister* was shortlisted for the Flash 500 competition, published by The Yellow Room online journal, the 2014 Café Lit Anthology, and online as part of Flash Flood Journal (National Flash Fiction Day, June 2013).

hour of the weekly visit. While Peter became Black Pete, Pirate Captain of the vegetable patch, to tempt the twins outdoors for fresh air and vitamin D. Giving Judy time to bond with their new granddaughter.

Silly old goat.

Her words still smarted. 'Why do you love me?' Peter had growled, fumbling socks over saggy feet. And she'd called him a silly old goat.

Judy's hip bumps his naked buttocks as she bends to the floor. Her back is smooth, dotted by a familiar map of honey freckles.

But Judy wouldn't have said goat. What had she called him? Silly old …

Silly old fox.

Silver fox was her pet name. When Peter's raven hair retired, he grew accustomed to (and secretly admired) his distinguished slate-grey look.

Peter entwines one leg around her lower calf to anchor himself before stretching fingers towards the needle on the mat. Judy's skin smells warm, he thinks of baked apple spiked with cinnamon. The terror of losing words engulfs him like seawater; an ice-cold wave strips away the façade of youth, exposing the crumpled reality of age beneath.

Judy's nipples precociously protrude, demanding his attention. Peter thinks of strawberry sauce dripping over dollops of cream. What had she promised to make him? The gooseberries were almost ripe.

Gooseberry fool.

Silly old fool.

That's what she'd called him, her eyes sparkling, bright with love.

He is an old fool. Not to remember why she loves him. She loves him for all the myriad of reasons that he loves her. And he loves her because she still wants to play Twister on Thursdays once their daughter has collected the grandchildren.

Peter's thigh trembles and he topples backwards to thump onto the sticky plastic sheet. Judy lands on top. They lie together, wrapped in giggles. She traces her finger along a line of grey hairs, moving down his body. Even the stabbing press of the Lego brick cannot block his growing desire.

'Gin and tonic?' Judy murmurs.

'Shall we take them upstairs?' says Peter.

His wife, of forty-eight years, smiles like a coquette. 'Well, it is Thursday.'

Nguyen Phan Que Mai

NGUYEN PHAN QUE MAI writes in both Vietnamese and English. She is the author of eight books of poetry, fiction and non-fiction. Que Mai has won some of the most prestigious literary awards of Vietnam, including the Poetry of the Year 2010 Award from the Hanoi Writers Association, the Capital's Literature & Arts Award, First Prize - the Poetry Competition about 1,000 Years of Hanoi, as well as the Vietnam Writers Association's Award for Outstanding Contribution to the Advancement of Vietnamese Literature Overseas. She is the first South-East Asian poet published under the prestigious Lannan Translations Selection Series. Her poetry collection *The Secret of Hoa Sen* (BOA Editions, New York, 2014) is said to build new bridges between Vietnam and America—two cultures bound together by war and destruction. The Los Angeles Review of Books, in their review of *The Secret of Hoa Sen*, called Que Mai 'one of Vietnam's foremost contemporary poets.'

Photo credit Vu Thi Van Anh

For more information about Nguyen Phan Que Mai and her works, visit her website:
www.nguyenphanquemai.com.en

Tears of Quang Tri[15]
qm1tea

AFTER THE LAST American soldiers
        had left Vietnam
        and grass had grown
        scars onto bomb craters,
        I took some foreign friends to
        Quảng Trị,
        once a fierce battlefield.

I was too young for the war
to crawl under my skin
so when I sat with my friends
at a roadside café, sipping tea,
enjoying the now-green landscape,
I didn't know how to react
when a starkly naked
woman rushed towards us, howling.

Her ribs protruded like the bones
 of a fish which had been skinned.
Her breasts swaying like long *mướp* fruit,

---

[15] First published by Terminus Magazine, a publication of Poetry@Tech, Georgia Tech University, Atlanta, Issue 11, 2014.

and her womanly hair a black jungle.

I was too young to know
what to say when the woman
shouted for my foreign friends
to return her husband and children to her.

Stunned, we watched her fight against villagers
who snatched her arms and dragged her away from us.
'She's been crazy,' the tea seller said.
'Her house was bombed.
Her children and husband …
she's been looking for them ever since.'

My friends bent their heads.
'But the war was here forty-six years ago,' I said.
'Some wounds can never heal.' The tea seller shrugged.

And here I was, thinking green grass
could heal bomb craters into scars.

Mrs Moreno[16]
qm2mrs

MEDELLIN, COLOMBIA.

THE kettle runs out of breath,
nursed back to life
by a pair of hands with skin
coloured by storms.

'There's no day I don't think about them,'
Mrs. Moreno says, her hands sing into the cup
filling it with the richness of her coffee.
Her words lead me
to the portraits of two handsome men— her sons.

'I thought I couldn't live on.'
She turns and hands me the cup.
 I feel her kindness
swell inside my throat;
she tells me about the bottomless
depth of loss
and what it means
to have both sons' lives
taken away by guns.

---

[16] First published by *Vietnam-US Magazine*, issue dated 12/6/2014

Mrs. Moreno holds my hands.
'Don't worry,' she says,
'I am okay. I have God's love.'
In her eyes, I find the light of truth,

and suddenly I am no longer
a stranger in a home
that smells like my grandmother's
even though
it is on the other side of the globe.

When Mrs. Moreno reaches
out to hold me to her heart
I hear faith
speak in a language
that needs no translation.

The Colour of Peace[17]
qm3pea

THE CHILDREN SURROUNDED themselves with chatter
that smelled like salsa, rising up
from their homes
that clung like bare bones to
mountain slopes.

Their parents and grandparents
stood
under a makeshift roof, telling me
how they had escaped bullets
that sprayed like rain
from helicopters twirling above their heads;
the children came to me, first as timid as cats,
and then they laughed,
rubbing their hands against the rough
silk of my Vietnamese dress.

My ears were still blurred by
explosions from the stories I'd just heard,
and my eyes still burned with tears
when the children reached up and took my hands.

---

[17] For the displaced people at La Cruz, Colombia. First published by Vietnam-US Magazine, issue dated 12/6/2014

They pulled me out to the sun,
And into the game of my faraway childhood hopscotch.
I jumped, bent, picked up
the pearl of laughter that giggled
out from their sun-roasted mouths,
and felt I belong here
to this land
torn by the civil war
and the evils of drugs.

As we sprung up
together, our footsteps light with hope
I knew the dead were watching over us,
and I saw how the colour of peace
turned into colour of laughter,
sung by the children of Colombia.

On Hanoi Street[18]
qm4on

HE WAS SO tall; when I looked up at him,
                in his eyes I wanted to see
                the Statue of Liberty
                bathed in the sunlight of his homeland.
                Instead, sorrow rolled down his face,
                trembling on his cheeks.

                "Mỹ Lai," he said, "I just visited Mỹ
Lai."
Then in his eyes, the photos he had seen there
at the site of the massacre came back:
a mother clutching her son in their deaths,
bodies of barefoot women strewn across muddy paths,
naked children, cold, and silent under the feet
of American soldiers who stood and smoked.

"You weren't involved." I shook my head. "It was the war."
Yet he trembled. It had taken him forty-two years to come back;
each of his days filled with nightmare
and the fear that some Vietnamese
would run him down with knives on the street.

---

[18] First published by Moving Worlds: A Journal of Transcultural Writings, 'Translating Southeast Asia' issue, Volume 15, Number 1, 2015

I wanted to say something else, but words didn't come,
so I pulled him into the stream of life
rushing around us: women balancing baskets of bursting flowers
on their slender shoulders, men cycling autumn away on their cyclos,
girls giggling their way to school, their áo dài dresses
fluttering like wings of white doves.

"This was a war zone when I left,"
he muttered as we passed
a group of boys who stood in a circle,
kicking a feathered ball to each other,
their laughter spiralling upward.
He jumped back as the feathered ball flew towards us.
"Kick it, Uncle, kick it," the boys called out to him in Vietnamese,
their arms stretching, pleading.

For a moment, he stood as if fear
had frozen inside of him.
The feathered ball dipped, spinning fast for the ground.
Suddenly his foot reached forward;
the ball was lifted
into sunlight.

Suzanne Conboy-Hill

DR SUZANNE CONBOY-HILL was a clinical psychologist for adults with intellectual disabilities for almost thirty years, working in NHS community services in London and Sussex. Latterly, as a writer of fiction, her observations of the impact of limited literacy on inclusion, communication, and exposure to the imaginings of others via written language led to thoughts about how that might be changed. This book is the result of one of those threads of thought. As a writer, she is a Lascaux Short Fiction Finalist, Flash Fiction Chronicles Finalist, and Best of the Net nominee. Her stories – some SF, some speculative, and some based in grim realism - have been published by Zouch Magazine, Full of Crow, Fine Linen Literary Journal, and the Lascaux 2014 anthology amongst others. She lives in the UK, holds degrees in several specialist areas of psychology and an MA in Creative Writing from the university of Lancaster. This is her website *http://www.conboy-hill.co.uk/*

Photo credit Michael Donne, Brighton
http://www.michaeldonne.co.uk/

Puddles like Pillows[20]
sch1lik

THINGS BEGAN DISAPPEARING ROUND about March. Just little things – a newspaper left on a bench, or a sandwich wrapper – and not blown away or tumbled into a corner, just gone. We shrugged collectively: so rubbish vanished - was that even a problem? Then somebody caught an empty beer can in the act and started squawking about it; how it went, like, straight up in the air, man, he said. Wasted, the rest of us said, because he wore big trainers and a hoodie. But almost overnight, YouTube was stuffed with videos of everything from paper clips to small toys vanishing into the sky. Just the ones left outside, mind; the ones indoors stayed put same as always.

After a while, with the streets and parks getting less cluttered, it started to look as if some cosmic recycler had dropped by to tidy us up. So then people stopped using the bins and just hung about with their cameras waiting for their banana skin or whatever to take off. Pretty soon, though, the yawn factor set in, what with the gazillions of uploads and the conspiracy

---

[20]First published in *Zouch Magazine*, 2013; Finalist and Best of the Net Nominee, the *Lascaux Short Fiction Prize*, 2014

theories, so eventually only little kids, grannies, and the seriously un-cool stuck around to watch any more. From there, it was only a small step to becoming a kind of unspoken utility and people began throwing litter out of their windows to save lugging bags and bins around. This meant you had to watch out for flying items which, when everybody got a bit blasé about it, could be anything from old phones to dead flower arrangements, some of them still in the vase. One man was killed by a sofa landing on him from the twenty second floor and its owner complained to the council about how it was their goddam fault because it never woulda happened if their goddam collection system hadn'ta broken down.

 We went on like this for quite a few weeks, with small inanimate objects on the outside of buildings heading skywards and everything else staying put. Then one day a miniature chihuahua was seen hovering at the end of its ten metre extending lead, yapping like they do and its owner yapping too, and people standing around hooting and yaw-hawing and filming it for posterity.

 This was about the same time NASA got involved, but it wasn't because of the chihuahua, it was because the ISS had been hit by a fountain pen, captured on video as it penetrated one of the external storage tanks. The gaseous discharge from the gigantic hole it left propelled the station out of orbit and now it was following Voyager into deep space with a trail of domestic debris behind it so it looked like a fourth grader's collage of a comet.

    Not long afterwards, bigger items like bikes and deliveries of wine in twelve bottle cases began disappearing straight upwards, and stuff that hadn't moved before because it was indoors, started bumping up against people's ceilings like birthday helium balloons. The ceiling became the go-to place for your missing credit cards and car keys, assuming you hadn't already lost those by leaving them to one side at a cash point or on top of the car roof at a filling station. For a while, the sky had been full of jangling black dots, clacking plastic that flipped and tipped and reflected the sunlight, and fluttering paper money birds. Now it was full of fridges, those big Marshall amps they have at music festivals, and parking attendants' huts that hadn't been fully bedded in.

    Chimney stacks, solar panels, large marquees, Smart cars, and Honda Civics went next, prompting a rush on the weightier Saabs, Four-by-Fours, and ex-army personnel carriers. Roofing experts worked over time, some of them entertaining the crowds by catching floating tiles and hammers while they hip-hopped along their scaffolding. And a new breed of specialist, claiming a hot line to The Rapture, started spamming everyone with texts about how, for a donation of only one thousand dollars, they could ensure you got a place in the light – never mind that it wasn't people that were vanishing, or that the Rapture-ists themselves were struggling to find a rationale that suited their purpose and had gone very quiet about it all.

When it rained, it rained very slowly and made puddles that looked like pillows.

People bought magnets, lead weights, and bits of cast iron and put them in anything moveable to keep it still. Old sea anchors were at a premium, and individuals carrying a bit of excess poundage hired themselves out to sit in things that might be vulnerable to a sudden uplift. One idiot tried to buy heavy water for his fish pond and got arrested as a terrorist. He'd still be on remand if it hadn't been for the jail disassembling upwards, brick by brick.

Once all the buildings and bridges were gone, along with the cattle and sheep and shrubs, and the boats and submarines and whales, there were only a few of us left – all clinging to trees that were slowly up-rooting, like we were in a massive flood with a current that was sucking everything along to some great overhead ocean.

For a while I had a kind of a neighbour; a woman in a purple skirt dangling upwards from a sycamore tree a few hundred yards away in what used to be our park. When it creaked and shattered and gave way, she went with it and I thought she'd yell or something but she didn't make a sound. I can't see anyone else now and I'm hanging here thinking I might be the last and wondering what I should say to mark the occasion: *So*

long and thanks for all the fish? Always look on the bright side of life (ti tum, ti-tum, ti-tum-ti-tum-ti-tum)? It ought to be something profound –
    Oh crap …

Albert's Teeth[21]
sch2tee

ALBERT'S TEETH ARE opinionated, unlike Albert. All day they clack on about things for which Albert has no interest or that he considers they should keep to themselves. It is especially difficult when they address the thorny question of what his wife looks like in a particular outfit. If they are complimentary, she will sidle up to him and make gooey eyes, and he is expected to make them back, as if they were sixteen again. Conversely, if they are not complimentary, supper is likely to be a very insular affair.

Albert often takes his teeth out at functions to avoid them insulting the vicar or the Lady Mayoress, but this means he cannot eat and so he has developed a strategy whereby he fills his mouth with as much food as possible and then eschews alcohol until he has been able to trap his teeth in a handkerchief in his pocket.

Albert always takes his teeth out at night to avoid opprobrium should they venture an opinion on his wife's upper aspect which has been making its way south for some years. This also means he can avoid any sex which

---

[21] Winner *West Sussex Writers'* Flash Fiction prize, 2015; published by *LA Review of LA*, June 2015.

might result from an inopportune comment. When once Albert's teeth said that they – not Albert of course – would like to slap Mrs Albert's backside until it glowed pink, Mrs Albert first slapped Albert around the face, and then presented him with her naked rump while giggling and cooing into the pillow.

    Albert puts his teeth in a glass on the night stand and seals them into it by placing a saucer on top. They natter and worry at him from there, sometimes gritted up tight, other times gaping like a hungry clam. One day, Albert thinks, he will put a stop to it all with a hammer.

Terminus[22]
sch3ter

HE TAKES THE Northern line, the doors whining and smacking as he sinks into a flashy neon seat; collar up, eyes down. A frown keeping the other eyes away. The Angel blows hot air as he leaves, whipping at his jacket with its stash of rumpled notes in the lining, cash jangling in the pockets like twanged nerves. The streets are slap wet, the steps steep. He steps deep, pushes the door and cracks it open. It's unmoored and adrift, leaking one world into another.

The room stinks; pinned-shut curtains, asleep on their makeshift wire, silently breathe in odours of dead food and trap them there. Some are well-nigh archaeological; foetid smears of smell that dwell between the bingeing threads of old cotton. Sly eyes watch, inviting communion: have a drink; have a smoke; chase a dragon.

Soft as a womb, this room. Blood warm, comfortable as a rush of sweet brandy on a winter's afternoon, warming fingers and toes and softening eyelids into a droop. He is where he is; a sloop safe in harbour, rising and falling on the swell, the sun over the yard's arm and nothing to say that hasn't been said a million times

---

[22] First published by *Fine Linen Literary Journal* January 2015

before. Veins squirm and flitting shadows worm needles into them, squeeze stuff down the tube and wait. Waiting is easy here where smoke hangs like old fog and no one cracks the tick-tocking silence.

    He shoots a line; jokes about riding out a shit storm and falls back on the smack-tacky sofa. It's a fine line, a rushing tidal line, and the ride feels free even though it isn't. The joker always pays in the end.

When Gliese Met Glasgow (and Muira made a mint)[23]
sch4met

MUIRA WAS A student linguist, a professional geek, and the only person to have communicated with the aliens directly. So when they suddenly appeared – not entirely coincidentally - in the sky over Glasgow, she became Earth's impromptu ambassador.

The aliens (who didn't think of themselves as such), were from a dense, parched, and much irradiated planet in the Gliese system (which they also didn't think of as such). As a consequence, they were short, swarthy, and extremely compact, and in the time it took to have a few radio exchanges with Muira via SETI, they figured out how to get here.

The politicians were not happy about Muira being Earth's poster girl. Black was ok, after all the aliens might be bright blue (ha ha ha); also Scottish (feisty lot, the Scots – you only had to look at Braveheart). But

---

[23] Finalist in the 2015 Coalition of Texans with Disabilities *Pen2Pen* competition.

female? Wouldn't proper First Contact diplomats expect to negotiate with men?

The aliens were not diplomats; they were traders-bordering-on-pirates because that was how their society worked. Find something everybody wanted and everybody was happy. They had no First Contact rules beyond haggling, although some of the preliminaries were not unlike the Glasgow Kiss and would come in handy later when they discovered football.

Another problem with Muira, the men in suits believed, was that she lacked stature, by which they meant height. Her clothes had to be specially made, table tops were inaccessible, and perched on a chair with her legs dangling, she was perpetually at risk of having her food cut up and fed to her on a spoon. But beggars could not be choosers so they had a business suit made for her, put cushions on her seat and a foot stool in the elevator so she could reach the buttons.

They forgot about the toilets which would themselves have benefited from the installation of one sort of stool in order to facilitate the depositing of another.

The aliens were very happy to see Earth (or *Zoclith,* as they called it) because it had commercial potential. The low gravity in particular was exhilarating. They rolled into squat little balls and bounced off the floor and ceiling of their guest quarters (a defunct but lockable nuclear bunker in the Highlands reputed to belong to the British Royal family).

When they were finally released from quarantine – which was just after they flooded the place upon discovering that Earth's water was an abundant commodity – the Gliesians bounded into the hotel conference centre and vaulted up into the vacant seats opposite the official welcoming committee. These were the first humans they had seen not encased in hazard suits, and they spent the next hour and a half doubled up laughing.

This was partly because the committee members reminded the Gliesians of the pale, stringy stuff they grew in caves and used for cleaning their teeth (think celery), and partly because their high pitched squawking sounded like swarms of copulating *pffidges*. The Gliesians themselves had very deep voices, the lower frequencies of which would have been of interest to orcas, had anyone thought to consult them.

Eventually, it occurred to someone to let Muira have a go, and she was deposited on the table in the middle of the 3D projection of a fish tank supplied as a de-stressor by a hostage negotiation company. Muira raised her arms above her head in greeting and the aliens stopped laughing. '*Fidge, pildex de-Zoclith* (We the People of Earth),' she said, with an exaggerated nod at the row of etiolated diplomats behind her, '*Scotle vish, pildex de-Praaxtol*, (welcome you, the People of Gliese).' She bared her teeth in a theatrical rictus. Then, suddenly conscious of appearing to be surrounded by guppies and probably looking as though she were drowning, she clasped her hands together and slowly brought them to rest on top of her head, for want of an immediately obvious alternative.

This modified gesture served to subtly transform the semantics of her message by slotting seamlessly into previously unexplained Gliesian mythology concerning powerful deities emerging from long-gone primal birth waters, so that what she actually said was, 'Kneel before me, for I am your Queen and I possess magic that will make you look like this lot (the celery) if you disobey.' They knelt.

In short order, Muira secured, in her own name, exclusive trading rights with Gliese; established a reality TV channel to follow the lives of people in Essex, parts of Cornwall, and the whole of America (ostensibly for cultural exchange purposes but really because the Gliesians had never laughed so much at anything before and would pay through the nose for it); and leased out the Moon as a bouncy castle for wedding parties.

Soon afterwards, with a hurriedly created Presidential Seal of United *Zoclith* (Earth), the *De-Praaxtol* (Gliesian) Ring of Perpetual Franchise, and a wadge of commercial contracts in her pocket, Muira left for a new life where she could look her subjects in the eye while she sold them box sets of *Dumb and Dumber*, *Last of the Summer Wine*, and anything featuring Prince Charles; and where it was possible to make all kinds of deposit without need of block and tackle.

The Collector[24]
sch5col

'ONLY ART IS immortal,' she says, her arms umber-stippled ribbons, lithe in the firelight. 'Humans are not.' Alia dances with cognisance, knowing every fluid move and bringing each one to him where he sits, red and heavy, in the warm desert sand.

'My passion is immortal,' he says to her. But he is a collector and he is thinking of how appreciative his friends will be of her exoticism. She will dance for them and their eyes will glow hot under the cold northern skies.

She makes an ululation, 'Humans grow old and they die,' she sings. Her words are bells somewhere within him, drawing together the scent of the smoke from the men's pipes, the bitter taste of the coffee on his tongue, and the pungency of the pack animals nearby. She is exquisite; he has bought her; he will take her home.

'There *is* another thing.' An older man, his breath smelling of liquorice, brings his face close so that his iron beard almost brushes the other man's *sgraffito* complexion.

---

[24] First published in the *Grievous Angel webzine* by Urban Fantasist, 2015.

'I have paid,' the collector replies, 'the contract is signed.' He slides a slow blink.

'A small ritual; our custom.' The old man inclines his head, smiles and weaves deference into the air with his hands. 'You will come?'

The night is filled with the heaviness of desert scents and the collector's mind with thoughts of Alia dancing to command. 'As you wish,' he agrees. So he, the old man, and Alia move away from the fire to a small tent; low hanging, tasselled, and lit with oil lamps. A bowl deep with henna sits in the centre and hollow brown pens surround it. A tattoo, he thinks. Well that can easily be removed.

But it is not for him. Alia turns away, letting her tunic fall to her waist, and now he sees that she is the embodiment of fine design – brown on gold, darker on dark, curving with her curves and extending tempting tendrils beyond the soft folds of her robe.

'Your likeness will appear here.' The old man indicates virgin skin towards the centre of Alia's spine and the collector leans close to look, excited by the intimacy of it. As he does, faint lines begin to appear – an outline, some shading – but with no stylus supplying the ink. He sits back: the drumming outside, the smoke, the spiced coffee – those things, he thinks, are playing tricks. He leans forward again, and now he notices human forms in the patterning. They are beautiful, but as he watches there is movement: eyes pleading, hands reaching out. Fear catches him and he sweats. Trickles of rose pigment erupt from his pores and fade to blush in salty streams, draining down from pastel shoulders, and bleaching the faint ink sketch that he is becoming until it holds nothing of him.

The new eyes on Alia's back deepen and weep.

'I told you,' she says, 'only Art is immortal.'

Ducks in a Row[25]
sch6row

THE DUCKS ARE in rows three across and four deep, waiting for the lights to change. The young man glances to his right and lightly depresses the accelerator; he will race away if the glance is returned and the vehicle worthy. But the driver is old and the car sedate so he waits, softens the engine, checks his mirror and waves back to friends in the car behind. They're going to the same place and they're travelling in a laddish two-car convoy aiming to get there at the same time.

The old man smiles to himself; he has just been kind and his journey today is a warm one for that reason and others. The sun is not melting the tarmac but it is making rolled-down windows and an elbow on the sill a summer pleasure after the days of rain. He glances left; in his younger days he would have given the laddie in the next car a run for his money when the lights changed. In his older days, he is content with some tuneless whistling.

Two cyclists weave to the front. Some disdain traffic lights but not these; they each put a foot down and

---

[25] In August, 2015, an air show jet ploughed into traffic waiting at lights on the nearby A27 in Shoreham, West Sussex, UK.

pause, taking in the brightness of the day, the summery whispering of the roadside trees, the midday blue of the sky, and the glinting rear windscreens of vehicles that got lucky by arriving at green. They are well on their way now to shops, the beach, grannies or aunties waiting to be taken for a pub lunch. The air has a slightly metallic tinge to it, of fuel maybe. Someone's engine needs adjusting.

The men in the row behind pass sandwiches between them; it may not be possible to eat when they get where they're going. They salute a can of fizzy drink at the windscreen but their friend up ahead doesn't see it. He is looking in his rear-view mirror once again but the shiny can is not as important as the dark shape in the sky that is looming and growing and makes no sense.

The driver to his left sees it too and his brain throws up words such as 'thrill', 'danger', and 'excitement', which seem to apply but in the exact moment in which he sits, feel somehow wrong and inadequate.

The people at the roadside are about to cross but with their ears unhindered by cocoons of glass and metal stuffed with airbags, or the clamouring streams of noise coming from in-car entertainment systems, they stop and look up. There is impossibility in the sky accompanied by roaring, shrieking, and not enough space left between its world and theirs. Some run; others are transfixed because of the words that push reality away - *these things do not happen.*

       The traffic lights are extinguished amid a greater brightness. Red and amber but not green.

       The tarmac boils and burns billowing black.

       There are no ducks at the oncoming lights, only witnesses.

Phillippa Yaa de Villiers

PHILLIPPA YAA DE VILLIERS is an award-winning South African writer and performance artist. The daughter of an Australian mother and a Ghanaian father, she was given up for adoption at nine months of age, although she was not told of it by her adoptive parents, a white family in apartheid South Africa, until she was 20 years old.

Phillippa studied journalism at Rhodes University, Grahamstown, and obtained a degree in Dramatic Art and Scriptwriting from the University of the Witwatersrand, South Africa. She is a graduate of the Lecoq International School of Theatre in Paris, France, and holds an MA in Creative Writing from the university of Lancaster. In 2014, Phillippa performed her specially commissioned Commonwealth poem in the presence of Queen Elizabeth II at Westminster Abbey. She currently teaches creative writing at Wits university. See more at: *http://www.poetryarchive.org/*

Photo credit Graham Mort

Night Fishing with Daddy[27]

pyv1fis

WE TURN OFF the national road, bump-bump-bumping through the veld, till we arrive at the great wet eye of the dam. The sun is low but it's still light. We unpack the truck. I've brought a friend along, she's thirteen to my aspirant twelve. While daddy puts up the tent, we play shyly around the water's edge. She's Italian, not used to camping or the outdoors. Her brand new tackies sparkle against the wild grasses. Two boys swim across the dam to talk to us. They ask if we are models. My eyes are full of my friend: she's so sophisticated, the way
she laughs at boys. Daddy prepares the rods and the bait. I am self-conscious. I don't want her to see how expertly I can hook a worm.

Our favourite fish are sweet-fleshed kurper and carp. We use worms for carp. Kurper prefer lumps of bread or mielie pap flavoured with custard powder or curry. We grasp the rods and follow daddy's movement, and cast. Listen to the long song of the line
as it flies over the water, then the plop as the

---

[27] First published in *The Everyday Wife*. Modjaji Books, 2019.

bait-laden hooks hit the surface, and we
girls giggling. Three times: song, plop,
giggle,

s o n g   plop giggle

s o n g p lop   g i g g l e.

Daddy lights the lantern. Boredom nibbles at our minds. A wild bird bustles noisily through the reeds, finding its nest. I steal a look at my friend. She sits passively as the shadows come to lie around her like old pets. I am mortified: she must be hating this. Teenagers should not be forced to go fishing. Worm-like I resent, struggling against the hook; then the darkness claims me,

I surrender to night
expectant as the water
holding secrets in its mouth

like babies

Bones[28]
pyv3bon

WHAT SHE KNOWS is what she remembers:
                      her mind field   a kraal of sanity
                      with a barrier of thorns
                      to keep her safely in.

                      In the cracked triangle of mirror she
                      searches her face
opening the drawers of eyes, lifting the soft texture of cheek
and chin to find what was left within, memories are
buried in her flesh like bones, but she cannot see them
now.

When she sleeps her skeleton stands up and paints her life.
Again, the hand covers the blackboard with poetry, and her story roams
between the growing minds of her students; love waits at the door
ready to carry her books home and children, eager for life
burst out of her womb and run to the laughing river.

---

[28] From the *Berlin Poesiefestival international anthology* 2012.

Her son is a stranger who comes on Sundays.
After lunch, he takes her for a walk.
The silence between them is littered with bones.

Breastsummer[29]
pdv4sum

AT FIRST I barely noticed you:
        the darker skin,
        the double kiss of nipples,
        dot dot
        adorning the free state
        of my flat brown
        little-girl body.

Like buds that swell in spring,
my body opened, a flower –
handfuls ripened to cupfuls,
then the full bounty
of my own, home-grown
life support system
ran over,
a breastsummer,
showcasing potential
suitors collected like coats and shoes,
I wore their eyes,
accessorised my self-esteem.

Only, in a mirror framed by shame
I named you: inadequate

---

[29] First published in *The Everyday Wife*. Modjaji Books. 2010.

uneven
too big
too small
ugly.

This body curves
around creation,
it is the work of mighty nature.
It is my land:
I live here.
I rename the elements these days;
I farm in phrases:
beautiful, holy, vital, divine,
warm, fertile, nurturing, mine.
Sky-seasons pass and I keep turning
the sweet earth,
planting hope in even furrows,
savouring the harvest.

Rapture[30]

pyv5rap

WE HAVE TO keep going as if there is a future, but it's the end of the world,

the rapture, screaming bodies hurled to heaven. Wars everywhere and the middle

east burning: the smell of bodies lost to wonder, the callous mistake of statistics

sunburnt holes in the sky and the ritual murder of elephants and rhinos

almost industrialized, like our responses   as automatic as breathing

as automatic as pressing a button   as automatic as autopilot settings

as bodies kept alive by machines, and we are asked what we think

like/don't like and there's the debate and the edge of the world subsides

---

[30] First published in the 2013 anthology *For Rhino in a Shrinking World* (Ed Harry Owen).

into flames of not caring. The world will end and we are
nowhere near

the ones we love and the cold voice of the airport tells us
to hurry to our boarding gate;

the ark is only half-built, the launch of the new strategy
for the state is still waiting

for a coat of paint.

Here's our life spread out in Eliot's etherized surgery,
facing Soyinka's unwelcome guest

who won't care about whether or not it's convenient for
you, will come calling when he likes

and when death comes for me I want to be busy making
light. It won't do to blame politicians for

power failures, I thank them as I write you, poem, into
life. Not

dead yet, I've still got the whole night because I am not
the one who was shot, banned or

almost beheaded, I am not the victim of some gruesome
experiment with power, I simply

stand and stare at our world and write down what I see
and even though it is misunderstood

at times, it stands.

The world ended just a moment ago

for another rhino lying in its lonely blood but that might not be on the news tomorrow.

Probably not. The news is hardly ever of sorrow but of egos mortally offended, naked

emperors and a child's laugh as he paints the funfair of history. The electricity of connection

fails to resurrect our community, we're in the dark here, so take this small hand,

this poem, this picture, spark stolen

from a power failure in Johannesburg:

may it light your way till you find your own.

Origin[31]

pyv2ori

TONIGHT, MY SON, my favourite poem,
                shares my bed. His gentle snores,
                like footprints on the night.
                He is upside down. What dream
                is holding him
                by the ankle?

                It has been two weeks and 10 000
miles,
our skins and eyes separated
from one another. Mothers and
their sons inhabit each other differently,
we are more than milk we are also
bread and the law and desire. I know that
I am his home as much as he is
my shelter. I am an expanding house,
growing taller as he reaches past me for
his own life.

Che Guevara changed the world for me, he was
some mother's son who dreamt a fairer future.
Our breakfast is our ideals, what we want
the world to be. Most important of the

---

[31] First published in *The Everyday Wife*. Modjaji Books. 2010.

meals, and life, the greatest prize, we fight
in trenches to defend its sovereignty.
This is how I was born in blood and
pain and mortality, my mind bright
laughing up to wish for more, and force
my tired feet against the discouraged hill,
and harness my rage and ride it home to change,
and still return to that first poem that called me
Mama.

Credits

Suzanne Conboy-Hill
Voice files: recording and post-production by Simon Walker of *Loophole Studios*[32], Brighton, UK. *Dorothy Rosser*[33], voice coach, Brighton, UK.

Tracy Fells
Voice files: recording and post-production by Simon Walker of *Loophole Studios*, Brighton, UK

Lyn Jennings
Voice files: recording and post production by Simon Walker of *Loophole Studios*, Brighton, UK

Nguyen Phan Que Mai
Voice files: recorded on iMac using Quicktime software. Post-production by Simon Walker of *Loophole Studios*, Brighton, UK.

Anne O'Brien:
Voice files: recorded on iPhone with post production by Simon Walker of *Loophole Studios*, Brighton, UK.

---

[32] *http://www.theloophole.co.uk/*
[33] *http://www.thevoicebox.org.uk/*

Phillippa Yaa de Villiers
Voice files: Licences granted by *Poetry Archive*[34] for re-use of audio files for *Origin, Breastsummer,* and *Bones*. Recording and post production of *Rapture* and *Night Fishing with Daddy* by Jurgen Meekel.

CREDIT AND MUCH gratitude also to all the first publishers who responded with alacrity and goodwill to requests for the inclusion of pieces here. In one instance, despite extensive searches the original publication could not be traced and the publishers were unresponsive. The author is clear that they retained the rights to republish but we apologise if we have been mistaken in this.

---

[34] http://www.poetryarchive.org/